Dream songs  Night songs
FROM BELGIUM TO BRAZIL

Around the world, the children sleep. Around the world, stars twinkle beside the smiling moon. En todo el mundo, los niños duermen. En todo el mundo, las estrellas brillan y la luna sonríe. Partout dans le monde, les enfants sommeillent. Partout dans le monde, les étoiles brillent et la lune sourit.

Let yourself get carried away
by a masked friend
Déjate llevar por un amigo enmascarado
Laisse-toi emporter par un ami masqué

In a dream where
you can taste everything
En un sueño donde podrás saborear todo
Dans un rêve où tu pourras tout savourer

**Follow in the footsteps
of an old woman**
Seguirás el camino que te marcó una viejita
Tu suivras le chemin tracé par une vieille dame

Towards a young musician
and his talking accordion

Hacia un músico joven y su acordeón que habla

Vers un jeune musicien et son accordéon parlant

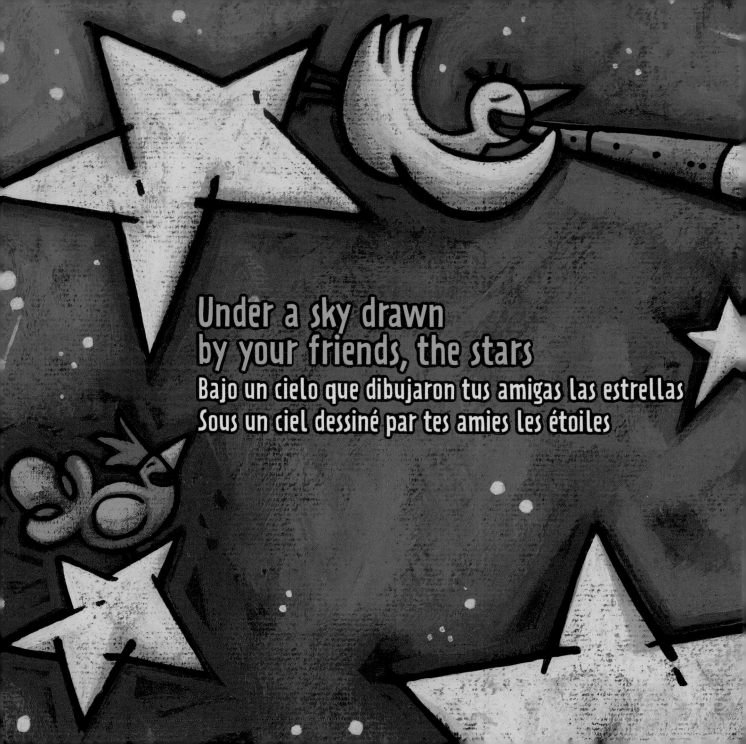

Under a sky drawn
by your friends, the stars
Bajo un cielo que dibujaron tus amigas las estrellas
Sous un ciel dessiné par tes amies les étoiles

You'll discover flowers
in the distance
Descubrirás las flores a lo lejos
Tu découvriras les fleurs dans le lointain

Humming a sweet tune for you
Que te tarareará un suave canto
Qui te fredonnera un doux refrain

The song of a sailboat
married to the sea
El del velero que se une al mar
Celui du voilier qui marie la mer

Dream songs  Night songs

1 Nade gau

INDONESIA • INDONÉSIE

Traditional, Arrangement Paul Campagne Collected by Francis Corpataux (Le chant des enfants du monde, Volume 4, Arion Music) Singers Hart-Rouge (Paul Campagne, Suzanne Campagne and Michelle Campagne)

Sleep, beautiful child, so your parents can work in the garden and grow food for you to eat.

Duerme, niño bonito, para que tus padres puedan trabajar en el huerto y darte de comer.

Endors-toi, bel enfant, sinon tes parents ne pourront travailler dans le jardin et te donner à manger.

2 Acalanto

BRAZIL • BRÉSIL

Lyrics and music Dorival Caymmi Singer Bïa

Bull, bull, bull... the bull with the black face holds his daughter, who is frightened by his mask.

Toro, toro, toro... el toro de cara negra sostiene a su hija que le teme a su máscara.

Bœuf, bœuf, bœuf... le bœuf au visage noir tient sa fille qui a peur de son masque.

3 Diarabi

SENEGAL • SÉNÉGAL

Traditional, Arrangement Zal Idrissa Sissokho Singer Zal Idrissa Sissokho

You must take care of all those you love; otherwise, you might hurt them.

Hay que cuidar a todos nuestros seres queridos, para no causarles dolor.

Il faut prendre soin de tous les gens qu'on aime, sans quoi, on peut causer de la peine.

4 Fais nanan m'tchou

BELGIUM · BÉLGICA · BELGIQUE

Traditional, Arrangement Paul Campagne Collected by Francis Corpataux
(Le chant des enfants du monde, Volume 12, Arion Music) Singers Hart-Rouge
(Paul Campagne, Suzanne Campagne and Michelle Campagne)

Sleep and later you can eat your fill.

Duerme, y después, podrás comer bien.

Fais dodo et plus tard tu pourras bien manger.

Atas Atas Amimmi

ALGERIA · ARGELIA · ALGÉRIE

Traditional, Arrangement Paul Campagne Singer Lynda Thalie
Preceded by the traditional tale Win rahou mâizatek? (Where have your goats gone?)

This one is little and wise. (the little finger) This one wears rings. (the ring finger) This one is large and wild. (the middle finger) That one licks the pot. (the index finger) That one crushes the little flea. (the thumb) Oh, old lady! (opening the child's hand) Where have your goats gone? There... there... there... or there? (pointing at parts of the body to be tickled) I'm the ant, I'm the mouse, I'm the old lady lighting her fire!

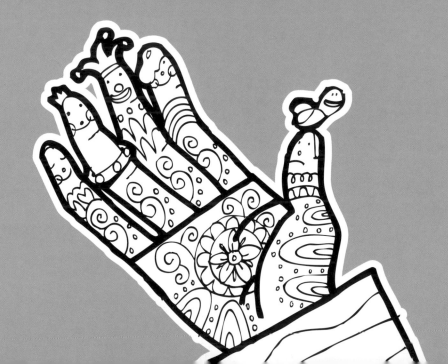

This one is little and wise. (the little finger) This one wears rings. (the ring finger) This one is large and wild. (the middle finger) That one licks the pot. (the index finger) That one crushes the little flea. (the thumb) Oh, old lady! (opening the child's hand) Where have your goats gone? There... there... there... or there? (pointing at parts of the body to be tickled) I'm the ant, I'm the mouse, I'm the old lady lighting her fire!

Éste es pequeño y quieto. (el meñique) Éste lleva anillos. (el anular) Éste es alto y loco. (el dedo mayor) Éste lame las ollas. (el índice) Éste aplasta el piojito. (el pulgar) ¡Oh, viejita! (al abrir la mano del niño) ¿A dónde se fueron tus cabritos? ¿Por aquí... por acá... por ahí... o por allá? (al indicar las partes del cuerpo del niño que provocan cosquillas) ¡Soy la hormiga, soy el ratón, soy la viejita que prepara su fogón!

6 Tumbalalaika

ISRAEL · ISRAËL

Traditional, Arrangement Paul Kunigis and Paul Campagne Singer Paul Kunigis

**Should a young man declare his love?
Will she accept him? Will she reject him?**

El jovencito debería declararle su amor?
¿Aceptará? ¿Lo rechazará?

Un jeune homme devrait-il déclarer son amour?
Acceptera-t-elle? Refusera-t-elle?

7 O Séy'a

CAMEROON • CAMERÚN • CAMEROUN

Traditional, Arrangement Paul Campagne **Singer** Muna Mingole

8 Breçairòla per la nena

OCCITANIA • OCCITANIE

Lyrics Louisa Paulin Music Daniel Loddo Singer Luc Lopez

We will not tell our little girl, who sings like the birds, that our heaven is in her eyes.

No le diremos a nuestra hijita, que canta como los pájaros, que nuestro cielo está en sus ojos.

Nous ne dirons pas à notre petite fille, qui chante comme les oiseaux, que notre ciel est dans ses yeux.

9 C'est la nuit mon petit ange

CANADA

Lyrics and music Michelle Campagne Singers Hart-Rouge
(Paul Campagne, Suzanne Campagne and Michelle Campagne)

Your ancestors are all there; they've passed beyond the stars.

Todos tus ancestros están allá,
más allá de las estrellas.

Tes ancêtres sont tous là et sont passés déjà
au-delà des étoiles.

10 Die blümeleine sie schlafen

GERMANY • ALEMANIA • ALLEMAGNE

Traditional, Arrangement Paul Campagne Singer Suzanne Campagne

Sleep like the little flowers and the sandman will not come.

Duerme como las florecitas,
y el ladrón no te llevará.

Dors comme les petites fleurs, et le marchand de sable ne viendra pas.

11 Dodo pti baba

SEYCHELLES

Traditional, Arrangement Paul Campagne Collected by Francis Corpataux
(Le chant des enfants du monde, Volume 4, Arion Music) Singer Muna Mingole

12 'Ndormenzete popin

ITALY • ITALIA • ITALIE

Traditional, Arrangement Marco Calliari Singer Marco Calliari

Between your cries I must work; but if you sleep, my treasure you'll be.

Entre tus gritos, tengo que trabajar, pero si descansas, serás mi esperanza.

Entre tes cris, je dois travailler, mais si tu t'endors, tu seras mon trésor.

13 We are the boat (Somos el barco)

UNITED STATES • ESTADOS UNIDOS • ÉTATS-UNIS

Lyrics and music Lorre Wyatt Singer Penny Lang

The river sings to the sea, the sea sings to the boat that carries us.

El río le canta al mar, el mar le canta al barco que nos lleva.

Le rivière chante à la mer, la mer chante au bateau qui nous porte.

Record Producer Paul Campagne Artistic Director Roland Stringer Recorded by Paul Campagne at Studio King Mixed and mastered by Davy Gallant at Dogger Pond Music Illustrations Sylvie Bourbonnière Story Patrick Lacoursière Spanish translation Service d'édition Guy Connolly Design Stephan Lorti for Haus Design Communications

SINGERS Luc Lopez Breçairòla per la nena Marco Calliari 'Ndormenzete popin Penny Lang We are the boat (Somos el barco) Muna Mingole Dodo pti baba, O Séy'a Zal Idrissa Sissokho Diarabi Paul Kunigis Tumbalalaika Bïa Acalanto Lynda Thalie Atas atas amimmi Michelle Campagne C'est la nuit, mon petit ange, Nade gau Suzanne Campagne Die blümeleine sie schlafen, Nade gau Paul Campagne Fais nanan m'tchou, Nade gau

BACK-UP SINGERS Hart Rouge (Michelle Campagne, Paul Campagne, Suzanne Campagne) Breçairòla per la nena, Fais nanan m'tchou, C'est la nuit, mon petit ange Muna Mungole O Séy'a Davy Gallant O Séy'a Aleksi Campagne Tumbalalaika, We are the boat (Somos el barco) Mia Campagne-Gallant Atas atas ammimi

MUSICIANS Paul Campagne electric, acoustic and classical guitar, bass, upright bass, ukulele, percussions, mandolin, kalimba Davy Gallant acoustic and electric guitar, mandolin, percussions, ocarina, flutes Michel Dupire pandero, djembe, ganzas, berimbau, maracas, bongo, cascara, tumba, tambour d'argile, guiro, rebolo, dumbek, cow bells, bombo, anklung, chimes Gilles Tessier electric guitar (O Séy'a) Yves Desrosiers classical guitar (Acalanto, We are the boat) Luc Lopez accordion (Breçairòla per la nena) Zal Idrissa Sissokho cora (Diarabi) Lucio Altobelli accordion ('Ndormenzete popin) Marco Calliari classical guitar ('Ndormenzete popin) Michelle Campagne piano (C'est la nuit, mon petit ange) Caroline Meunier accordion (Tumbalalaika) Paul Kunigis piano (Tumbalalaika) Penny Lang acoustic guitar (We are the boat)

THANK YOU TO Patrick Cameron, Nick Carbone, Vincent Martineau, Gina Brault, Heidi Fleming, Henri Sylvain Wandji, Ulli Hetscher, Véronique Croisile, Patricia Huot, Mona Cochingyan, Connie Kaldor, Bernard Bocquel

Bïa appears courtesy of Les Disques Audiogramme inc. et de SONY BMG Entertainment France.

We acknowledge the financial support of the Government of Canada through the Canada Music Fund for this project.

(R) www.thesecretmountain.com

(C)(P) 2008 Folle Avoine Productions, Lac Laplume Musique
except Acalanto, Breçairòla per la nena et We are the boat (Somos el barco)